Mike Purewal

On Your Way!

Bumblebee Books
London

BUMBLEBEE PAPERBACK EDITION

Copyright © Mike Purewal 2022

The right of Mike Purewal to be identified as author of
this work has been asserted in accordance with sections 77 and 78 of the Copyright, Designs and
Patents Act 1988.

All Rights Reserved

No reproduction, copy or transmission of this publication
may be made without written permission.
No paragraph of this publication may be reproduced,
copied or transmitted save with the written permission of the publisher, or in accordance with the
provisions of the Copyright Act 1956 (as amended).

Any person who commits any unauthorised act in relation to
this publication may be liable to criminal
prosecution and civil claims for damage.

A CIP catalogue record for this title is
available from the British Library.

ISBN: 978-1-83934-417-6

Bumblebee Books is an imprint of
Olympia Publishers.

First Published in 2022

Bumblebee Books
Tallis House
2 Tallis Street
London
EC4Y 0AB

Printed in Great Britain

www.olympiapublishers.com

Dedication

To my dearest, sweetheart, Bianca. Since you were born, you owned my heart! Daddy loves you and is so proud of his perfect girl! I wish you a lifetime of adventure, fun and happiness. Love, always, your Dada!

Today is the day,
to be on your way!
Put down those toys,
that cause you to stay.
Turn off that tablet and TV,
turn on your mind and follow me!

With the sun shining bright,
you fly your magic kite,
with all your magic might.

Up

Up

Up

And away it will go,
staying not so low.
You try to catch up,
but move too slow.

It gets caught in a rainbow tree,
one so beautiful to see.
Flowers grow each and every way,
with animals coming out to play!

But the workers with their saws,
start to chop, lips smacking their jaws.

You scream as loud as you can,
at Imran, Nathan and Keenan!
No one can stop what already began...

But no, not you.
Your heart shines through.
Compelled to do,
you kick up your shoe!

My dear friend, anger is natural to you and me.
Let's not sit in anger constantly,
as this may hurt us eventually.

Racing to the city, face burning red,
swerving the streets getting ahead!
Through the smog and fog,
it's hard to see dogs jog!
No one can hear you yell,
as everyone is in their shell.

Coming and going,
so fast without knowing.
To get here and there
and there and here.
Never to go anywhere!

To race then pace.
To rush then flush.
To jump then slump.
To speed then heed.

This way to run,
is not any fun.
Around and around …
Can it be undone?

Yes, you bravely say!
And want to be on your way.
What gets you out on a whip?
It's your very own rocket ship!

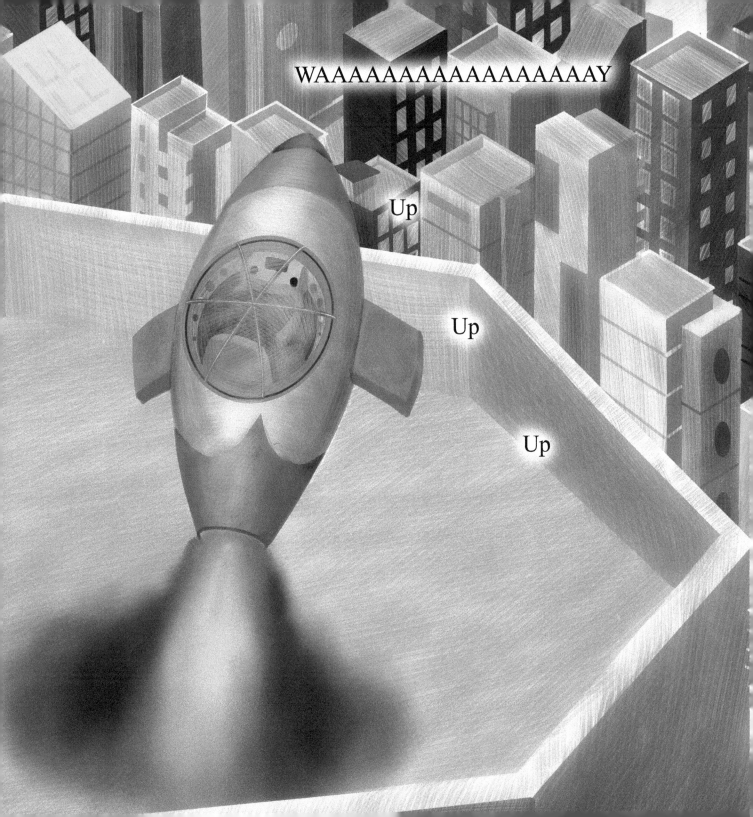

Oh what a sight this is to see!
Earth starts to disappear magically.
Over the moon that looked so small,
you're the captain making the call,
continuing to blast fast past it all.

The stars, with smiles on their face,
dance around, welcoming with grace.
They will put on a great show,
as your friends line up in a row.
You're all special, this they know!

With thumping beats,
you're in for a treat.
The great show starts,
without any feet!

The stars play it all
feeling like a magical ball
From guitars to sitars
From trombones to xylophones
From trumpets with thumpets

A bang is heard around Mars!
You say goodbye to the stars.
This adventure will continue,
you've come this far.

Travelling fast and a little upset,
wishing you had that tablet.
This mysterious planet is dark,
wanting to be at a park.

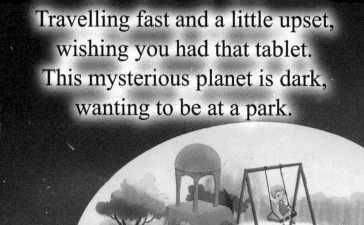

Needing this to quickly pass,
pushing the pedal, with your mass.
But the ship has run out of gas!

You land the ship so very right,
to look takes all your might!
Overcome with fright.

My dear friend, fear is natural to you and me.
Let's not sit in fear constantly,
as this may hurt us eventually.

Taking a step out,
with a whimper and pout.
Hearing sounds as you shiver,
knees buckle and quiver.
Kidneys wrapped around your liver!

Holding the pump,
your heart thumps.
But you are brave,
entering this gigantic cave!

Finding a murky lake,
the smell is hard to take.
The pump sucks up goo,
filtering gas coming through.
The machine spits out the junk,
getting you out of your funk!

Dancing to the ship,
you dare not slip.
Filling up the gas,
the ship roars with sass!

No longer wanting to roam,
and wishing to be back at home.

Seeing the ocean thinking fast,
knowing the ocean is so vast.
Landing with a big splash!
The ship is dented but not a total mash.

As you think,
starting to sink.
The ocean begins to grow.
Down you go, low low low…

My dear friend, worry is natural to you and me.
Let's not sit in worry constantly,
as this may hurt us eventually.

Where are you?
What will you do?
Arriving amongst the few,
and oh what a view!
For what it's worth,
it's the powers at the centre of Earth!

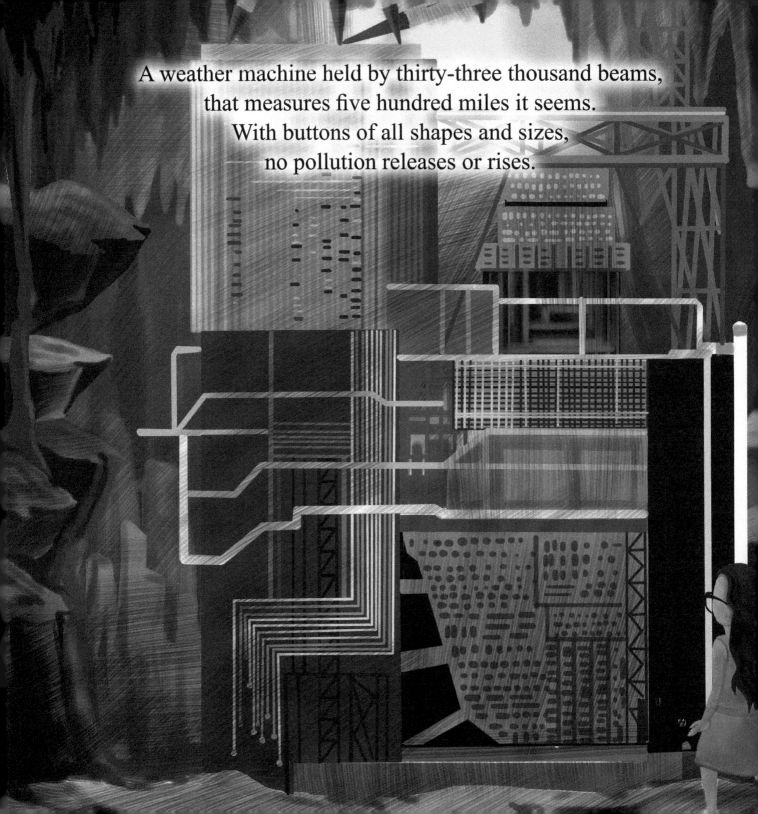

A weather machine held by thirty-three thousand beams,
that measures five hundred miles it seems.
With buttons of all shapes and sizes,
no pollution releases or rises.

As far as you can see,
are dials in synchronicity.
Making the sun set and rise,
which strained your eyes.
When you turned off the TV,
coming on this adventure with me!

Attached to the dial,
with all records on file,
is a twisty turn table,
using so many cables.
Making the Earth spin around,
tracking what goes up and down!

Like that rainbow tree chopped to the ground.
All the history here can be found.
When it was planted and how much it grew,
more seeding will create trees brand new!

Which will clear the fog,
to look up with no smog.
Watching the stars twinkle at night,
the great show will always live bright.

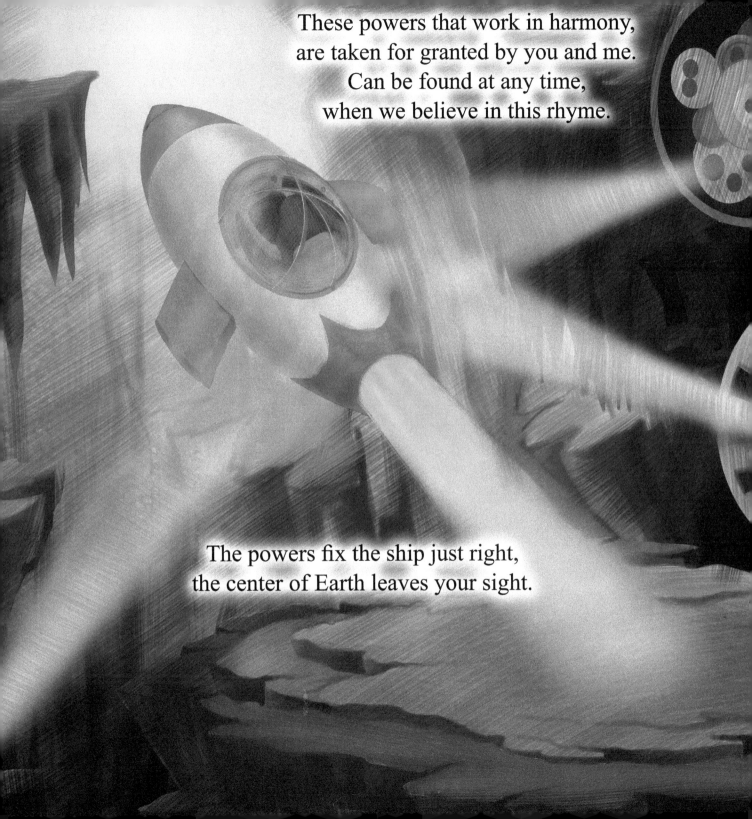

These powers that work in harmony,
are taken for granted by you and me.
Can be found at any time,
when we believe in this rhyme.

The powers fix the ship just right,
the center of Earth leaves your sight.

Back home with friends you met,
not picking up that tablet.
More adventures wait for you,
certainly not just one or two.

Make roads that are not yet paved.
My dear friend be courageous, be brave.
And with appreciation of today,
now you are on your way!

About the Author

Mike Purewal worked in corporate for twenty years culminating as a Vice President of Sales. Along the way, he took the road less travelled by unplugging and living in the majestic Redwoods in Northern California for a year, studying happiness, mindfulness and meditation. This experience radically changed Mike's outlook on life and he is now following his passion of writing children's books that inspire humour, creativity and imagination. His ultimate goal is to bring more laughter and joy to the world for both children and adults alike.

Mike currently lives in the greater Toronto area with his wife and daughter.

MIKEPUREWAL.COM
Instagram: @mike.purewal

CPSIA information can be obtained
at www.ICGtesting.com
Printed in the USA
BVHW021708281022
650569BV00023B/1479

9 781839 344176